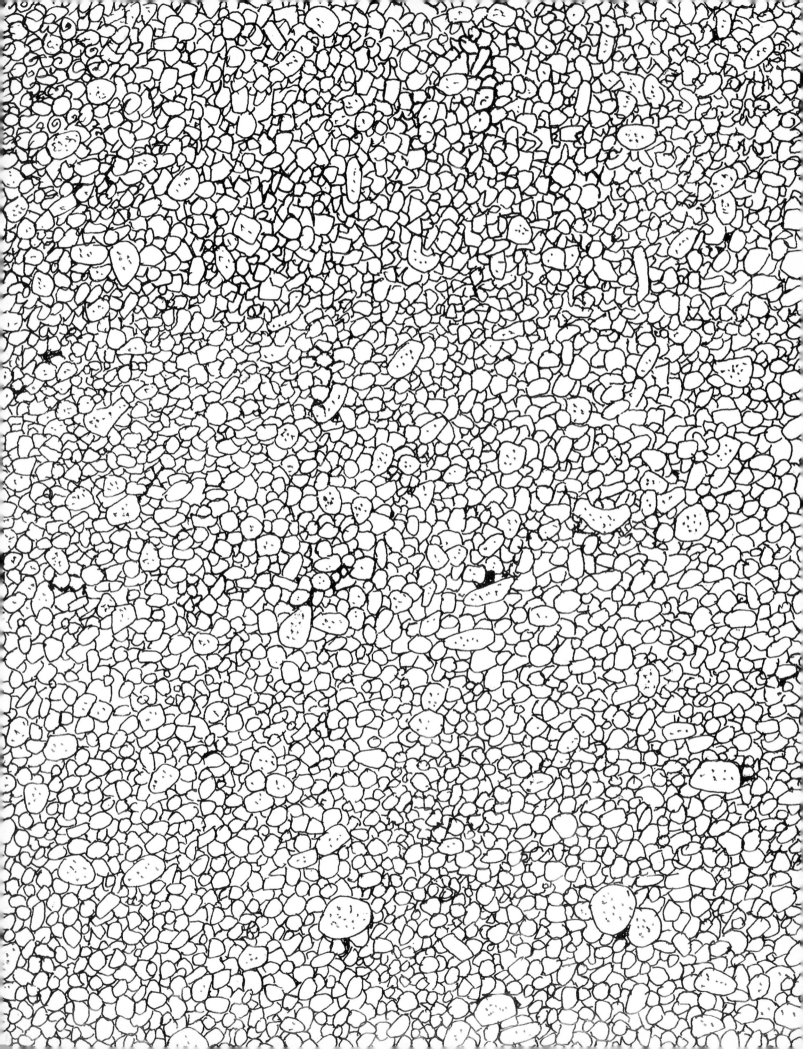

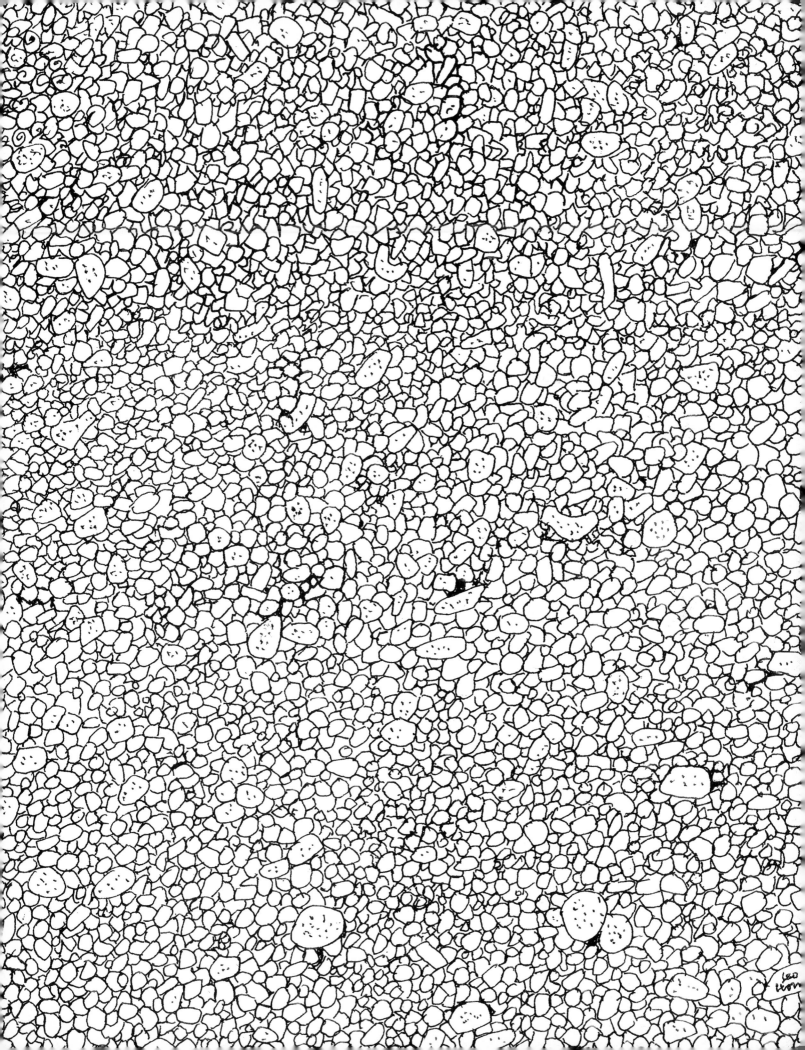

An Extraordinary Egg

by Leo Lionni

Scholastic Inc.
New York   Toronto   London   Auckland   Sydney

On Pebble Island, there lived three frogs: Marilyn, August, and one who was always somewhere else.

That one's name was Jessica.

Jessica was full of wonder. She would go on long walks, way to the other side of Pebble Island, and return at the end of the day, shouting, "Look what I found!" And even if it was nothing but an ordinary little pebble, she would say, "Isn't it extraordinary?" But Marilyn and August were never impressed.

One day, in a mound of stones, she found one that stood out from all the others. It was perfect, white like the snow and round like the full moon on a midsummer night. Even though it was almost as big as she was, Jessica decided to bring it home.

"I wonder what Marilyn and August will say when they see this!" she thought as she rolled the beautiful stone to the small inlet where the three of them lived.

"Look what I found!" she shouted triumphantly. "A huge pebble!"

This time Marilyn and August were truly astonished. "That is not a pebble," said Marilyn, who knew everything about everything. "It's an egg. A chicken egg."

"A chicken egg? How do you know it's a chicken egg?" asked Jessica, who had never even heard of chickens.

Marilyn smiled. "There are some things you just know."

A few days later, the frogs heard a strange noise coming from the egg. They watched in amazement as the egg cracked and out crawled a long, scaly creature that walked on four legs.

"See!" exclaimed Marilyn. "I was right! It *is* a chicken!"

"A chicken!" they all shouted.

The chicken took a deep breath, grunted, gave each of the astonished frogs a look, and said in a small, raspy voice, "Where is the water?"

"Straight ahead!" the frogs cried out excitedly.

The chicken threw herself into the water, and the frogs dove in after her. To their surprise, the chicken was a good swimmer, and fast too, and she showed them new ways to float and paddle. They had a wonderful time together and played from sunup to sundown.

And so it went for many days.

Then, one day, when Jessica was somewhere else, August and Marilyn saw a commotion in the water below them. Someone was in trouble. Quickly, the chicken dove into the dark pool. August and Marilyn were frightened.

After a few long moments, the chicken reappeared, carrying Jessica. "I'm all right," she called. "I got tangled in the weeds, but the chicken saved me."

From that day on, Jessica and her rescuer were inseparable friends. Wherever Jessica went, the chicken went too. They traveled all over the island. They went to Jessica's secret thinking place . . .

. . . and to the great pebble monument.

One day they went to a place where Jessica had never been before. A red and blue bird flew down from a tree.

"Oh, there you are!" it exclaimed when it saw the chicken. "Your mother has been looking all over for you! Come! I'll take you to her."

They followed the bird for a very long time.
They walked and they walked. They walked
under the warm sun and the cool moon, and then . . .

... they came upon the most extraordinary creature they had ever seen.

It was asleep. But when it heard the little chicken shout "Mother!"
it slowly opened one eye, smiled an enormous smile, and, in a voice as
gentle as the whispering grass, said, "Come here, my sweet little alligator."
And the little chicken climbed happily onto her mother's nose.

"Now it's time for me to go," said Jessica. "I'll miss you
very much, little chicken. Come visit us soon—and
bring your mother too."

Jessica couldn't wait to tell Marilyn and August
what had happened. As she neared the inlet, she
shouted, "Guess what I found!" And she told them all
about it. "And do you know what the mother chicken
said to her baby?" Jessica asked. "She called her
'my sweet little alligator'!"

"Alligator!" said Marilyn. "What a silly thing
to say!"

And the three frogs couldn't stop laughing.

ISBN 0-590-60699-9

12 11 10 9 8 7 6 5 4 3 2 1   5 6 7 8 9/9 0/0

Printed in U.S.A.   08

First Scholastic printing, March 1995

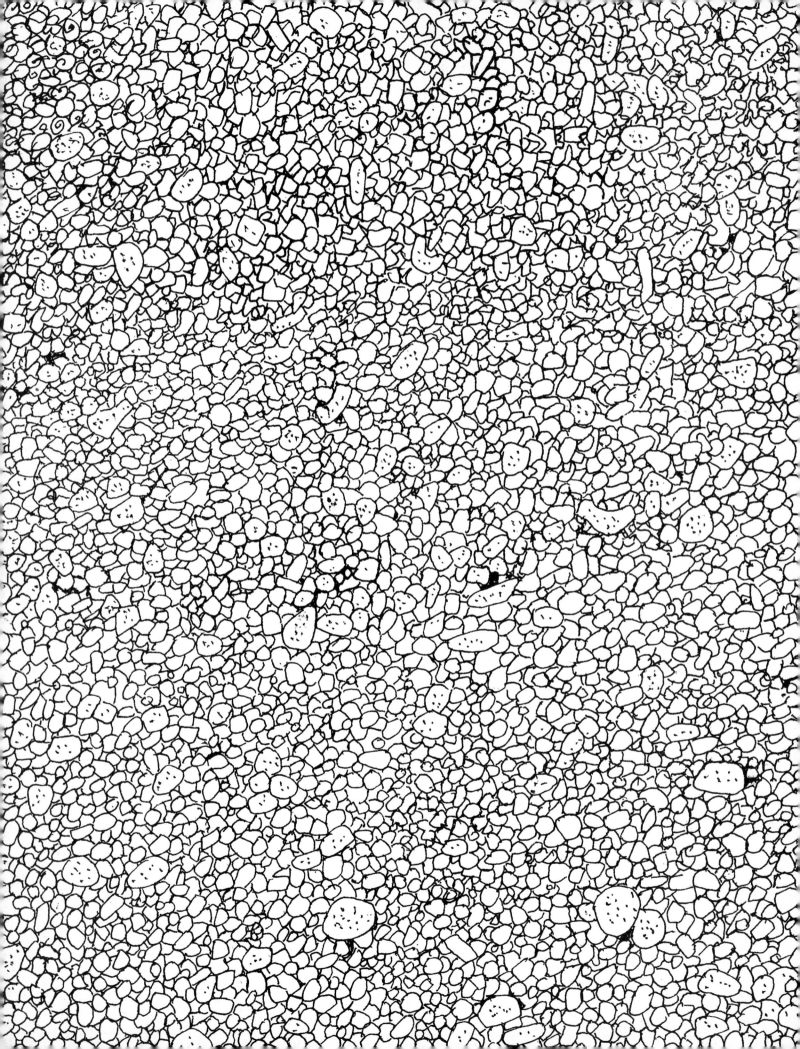

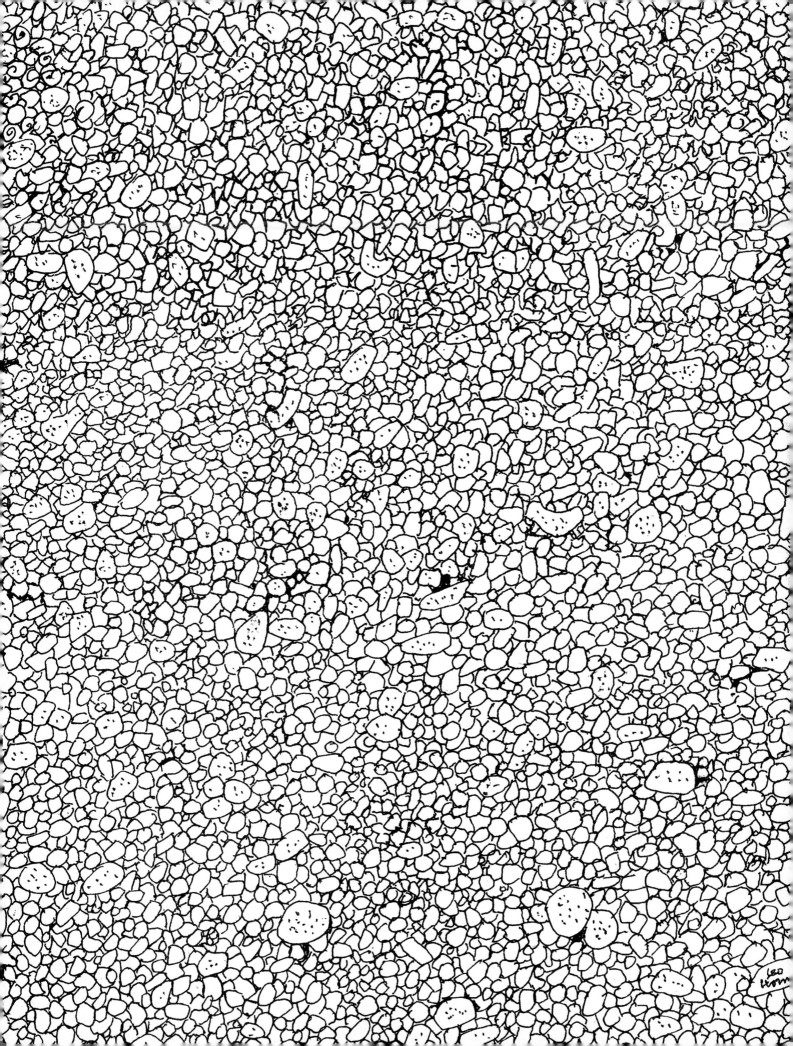